CINNAMON'S DAY OUT

~A Gerbil Adventure~

SUSAN L. ROTH

DIAL BOOKS FOR YOUNG READERS
NEW YORK

To Dale and Doug

Published by Dial Books for Young Readers
A member of Penguin Putnam Inc.
375 Hudson Street
New York, New York 10014

Designed by Ann Finnell
Printed in Hong Kong on acid-free paper
First Edition
1 3 5 7 9 10 8 6 4 2

Library of Congress Cataloging in Publication Data
available upon request

I would like to thank Cindy Kane
and her gerbil-owning family,
Ann Finnell, Alana Roth, the Sea Breeze Pet Center,
the Coral Reef Pet Shop,
and Shear Grace Pet Shop for their help.

In these collages I used real wood chips,
paper towel tubes, screen, wallpaper, and wood.
The cat is made of corrugated cardboard,
while Cinnamon, Snowball, and the other images
were all cut from papers I have collected,
including some fine pieces handmade by Suzi Zobrist
of East Sound, Washington.
The collages were then photographed by Gamma One,
and the color separations were made
from transparencies.

Snowball!

Cinnamon!

Where were you?
I looked everywhere!

I've been OUT!

This morning
you were sleeping,
but I was chewing, chewing, chewing,

I chewed until I reached the sky, and then . . .

chewing.

down it crashed!

I was on top . . .

of a mountain.

There were steps

leading to . . .

a city. Looking both ways,

I crossed the street and found . . .

a meadow. I nibbled

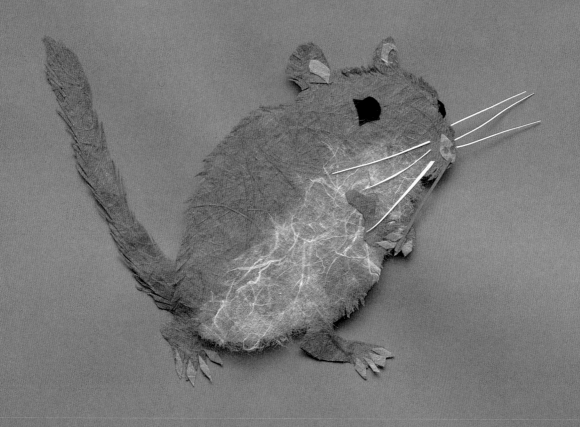

the grass until . . .

I saw a wolf!

I ran . . .

for the train

and rode . . .

far away.

A path led . . .

to a pond.

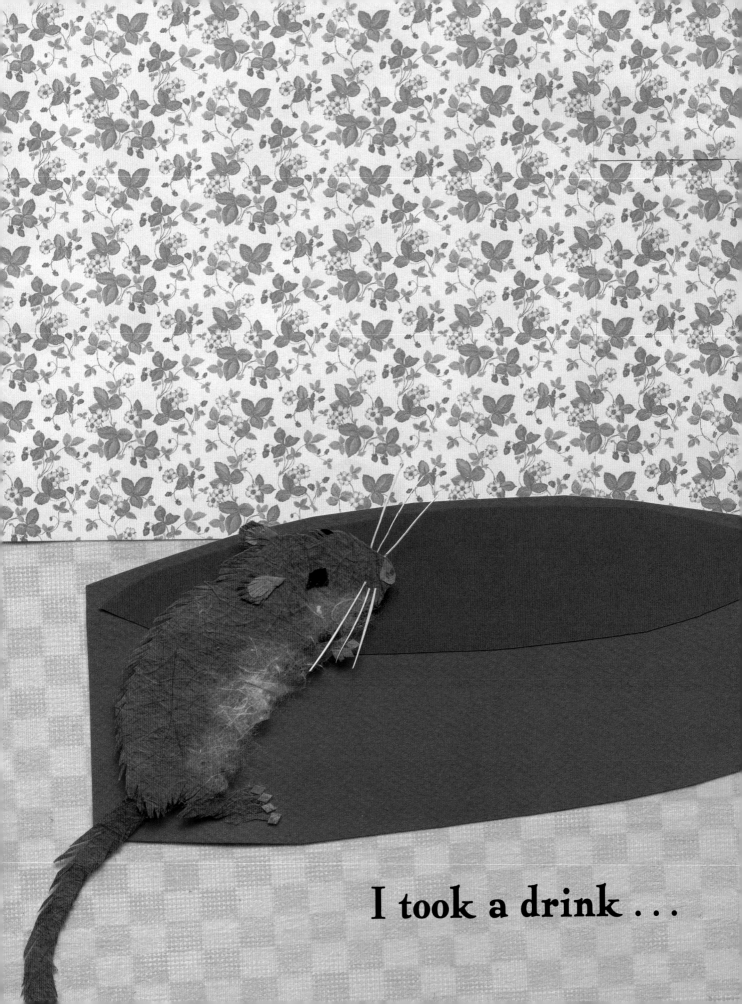

I took a drink . . .

but I met

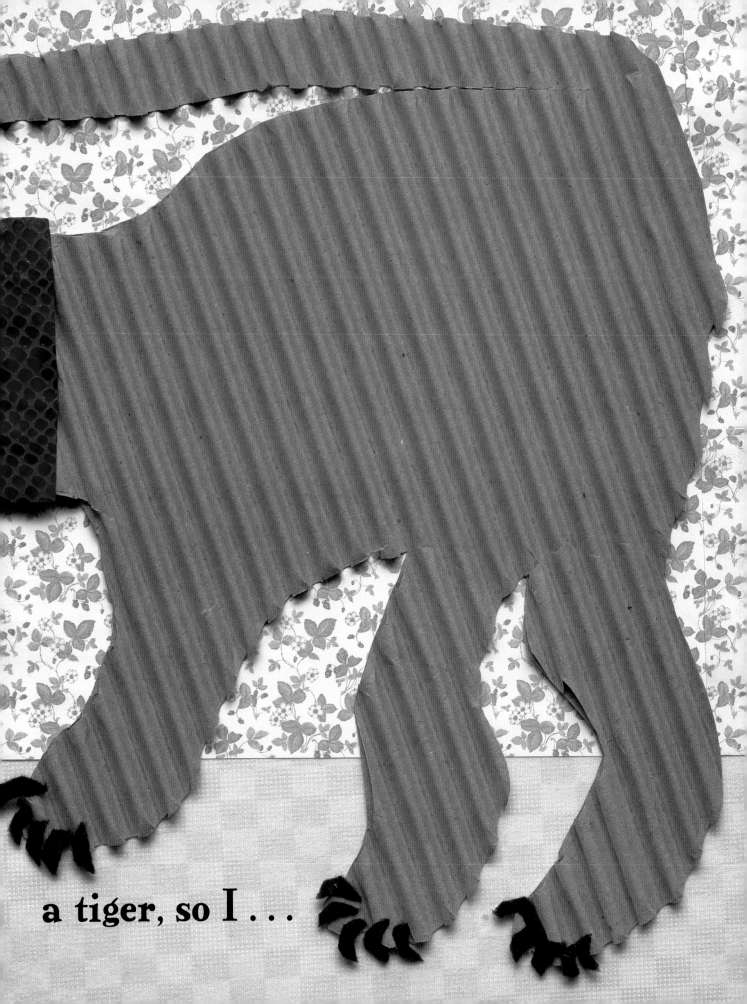

a tiger, so I . . .

hid in a barn,

and ate and ate until

the giant came. "Cinnamon!" it said.

"What are you doing in the cupboard?"

And then . . .

I flew . . .

over all I had seen,

until I came back . . .

home to you.

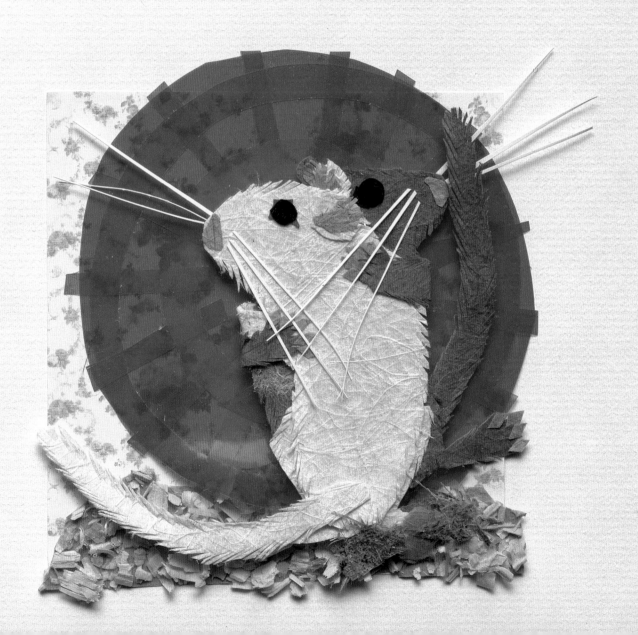